Written by
Karen Gedig
Burnett

Illustrated by
Laurie Barrows

Katie's Rose

**A
Tale of
Two
Late
Bloomers**

a grandma rose story

Tom & Renee
To remind all of
us to KEEP
Blooming!
Ka

GR Publishing • Roseville, CA 95661
www.grandmarose.com

Illustrations ©2000 Laurie Barrows

Cover design: Tamara Dever, TLC Graphics, www.TLCGraphics.com

Burnett, Karen Gedig.
        Katie's rose : a tale of two late bloomers/
author, Karen Gedig Burnett; illustrator, Laurie Barrows. -- 1st ed.
    p. cm.
    LCCN: 00-134955
    ISBN: 09668530-2-4 (hardback)
    ISBN: 09668530-3-2 (softback)
    SUMMARY: Katie's parents are concerned that she doesn't act as
mature for her age as they would like. Then one day Grandma Rose
takes them through her beautiful flower garden to show them a special
flower, a rosebud that will bloom some day, but can't be rushed--just
like Katie. Notes about people who were late bloomers follow the story.
    1. Maturation (Psychology)--Juvenile fiction. 2. Daughters--
Psychology--Juvenile fiction. 3. Parenting--Juvenile fiction. I. Barrows,
Laurie, ill. II. Title.

PZ7.B937Kat 2000   [E]
                         QB100-901205

10 9 8 7 6 5 4 3 2 1

Printed in Hong Kong

DEDICATED TO

Trevor, Caitlin, Gavin, Weston,
and all the different roses in the world.

When Katie and her
mother went for a jog,
they stopped to talk
to Grandma Rose.

They talked about the
garden and they
talked about
the weather ...

... and they talked about Katie.

When Katie and her father
took the baby for a stroll,
they stopped to talk to Grandma Rose.

They talked about the wind
and they talked about the trees ...

... and they talked about Katie.

When Katie and her friends went for a ride, they stopped to talk to Grandma Rose.

They talked
about the park and
they talked about their bikes ...

... and they did flips and tricks.

Grandma Rose laughed and gave
them cookies and punch.

When Katie and her family
went for a walk, they stopped
to talk to Grandma Rose.

They talked
about the rain
and they talked
about the
clouds ...

... and Grandma Rose said,
"Come, I want to show you something special
in my garden."

Grandma Rose walked past many beautiful flowers. Then she stopped. "Ah, here's one," she said as she reached out and cupped a new little rosebud in her hands.

"These rosebuds are special," she said, "because inside each one is a flower that will bloom some day."

"I can't make them bloom," said Grandma Rose.
"I just water them, and take care of them.
They will bloom when they're ready

... just like children."

Katie's mother and father
looked at each other.

Then they all turned to watch Katie.

Finally her father said,
"Well, we'd better get going."

"I have some potted roses," said Grandma Rose. "Katie, would you like to take one home?"

Katie nodded and slowly looked at all the plants.

Then she picked
the perfect one.
The plant that
had one tiny bud.

And Katie skipped
all the way home.

the end

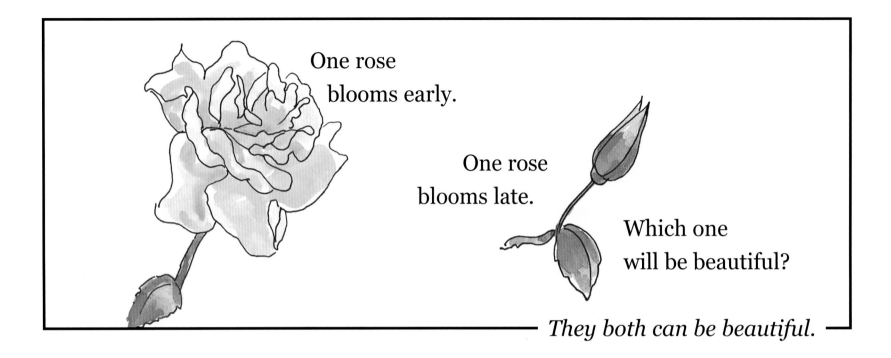

One rose
blooms early.

One rose
blooms late.

Which one
will be beautiful?

They both can be beautiful.

One tree
grows fast.
One tree
grows slow.

Which one will
be the best?

There is no best, they're just different.

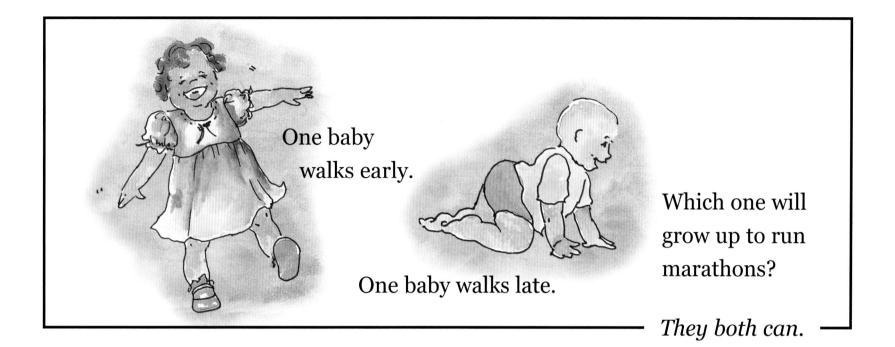

One baby walks early.

One baby walks late.

Which one will grow up to run marathons?

They both can.

One child reads early.

One child reads late.

Which one will grow up to do wonderful things?

They both can.

"We all bloom at different times,"
said Grandma Rose.
"Now use both of your
hands to make a fist."

"Then open them
to show how far you
think you've bloomed."

"Life is not a contest. It doesn't matter who blooms the FASTEST.
What does matter is that you KEEP BLOOMING."

People bloom at *their own* time:

ALBERT EINSTEIN

Albert Einstein was one of the smartest people who ever lived. But Albert didn't speak until he was 4 and didn't read until he was 9. He struggled in school and when he finally graduated he wasn't able to get jobs that he wanted. Albert didn't bloom until he was in his 20s.

GRANDMA MOSES

Anna Robertson Moses was a farmer's wife and a mother. She liked to sew. When she was in her 70s it became too hard for her to hold a needle, so she tried painting. When she was in her 80s people started buying her pictures. She became very famous. People loved her paintings. Grandma Moses painted almost 2,000 pictures before she died at the age of 101. She was a very late bloomer.

MICHAEL JORDAN

Michael is a great basketball player, right? Well, when he was in the ninth grade he was cut from the basketball team. There were other players who were better. In the tenth grade he made the team but still was not considered one of the best players. But he was blooming. By the middle of the eleventh grade people began to see that he was special.

KAREN GEDIG BURNETT

Karen was young for her age and never felt like she fit in. She struggled in school and with friends. She didn't get her first 'A' in school until she was 20 years old. By then she had 'caught up' with the kids her age and had many friends. Karen became a counselor and is the author of this book. (*P.S. She's still blooming.*)

Note to Parents, Grandparents, Teachers, and All Who Love and Care For Children:

Most of us realize that children bloom in their own time and in their own way. Then why is it sometimes so hard to restrain ourselves when we see a child struggle or stumble or even skip or dawdle toward the future? When we see them veer off a known path to success, it's hard to hold our tongue and our actions. We want so desperately for them to succeed. Often we already have a vision of what 'succeed' means. When children don't follow that path, or at least stay close, we become afraid: afraid they won't go somewhere, be someone, achieve their potential, keep up with others, prove something; afraid we are doing things wrong - or at least not doing them right. Our own fears get in our way of accepting them just as they are. Our own fears drive us to jump in and push, pull, and try to take control. We may even berate and criticize in our attempt to keep them on the path.

The truth is there are many paths to success. And success means something different to each person. Is it our success we are seeking, or theirs? Isn't our job to help them decide what success means to them and help them travel in that direction? Many marvelous things can be accomplished while traveling in unconventional directions.

That doesn't mean they won't at times need a nudge and maybe even a shove. We have all benefitted from timely interventions in our life. But is this an occasional occurrence or an ongoing pattern? Is it accompanied by a strong dose of support, encouragement and love?

Since there is such a delicate balance between guiding and pushing/pulling, here are some guidelines:

- **SUPPORT:** Support who they are. Remember, not only do our "roses" bloom at their own rate but they also bloom their own hue. We can't force them to go faster or to be something or someone they aren't. Instead, we need to celebrate who they are. Focus on their strengths and talents. Recognize and highlight their finer qualities. Hold out models for them to see how these qualities can benefit them as they grow.

- **RESPECT:** Respect their interests, their talents, their dreams. Treat them as you would want to be treated. Respect is a two way street, not a one way alley. Respect is also a learned behavior.

- **FAITH:** Have faith in them. Each color and kind of rose has its own beauty. Every child, every human, has a purpose, a talent, a value. Believe in them. They may go off in strange directions and you may not be able to envision where it will lead. Remember, too, there are many seasons in a lifetime. What may show little color in one season may be the grand champion of another. Have faith in them.

I have two very different roses, two boys, each with his own unique bloom pattern. It's not my role to decide who or what they will be, or judge which style or path has more value. My job is to nourish and encourage them. They will be **the best they can be** when I support **who they are**.

Karen Gedig Burnett
Karen Gedig Burnett
a.k.a. Grandma Rose

For more information visit:
www.grandmarose.com
Or contact: GR Publishing
P.O. Box 217, Roseville, CA 95678